Farmyard Adventures

Written by Graham Marks —— Illustrated by Manhar Chauhan

SIENA

Poppy Pig's Tight Squeeze!

As well as breakfast, lunch and dinner, Poppy Piglet always liked to have a little snack between meals to keep her going. "I want to grow up to be a lovely big pig one day," she said to her friend Paul, "so I need a little snack now and then." Paul looked at her and laughed, "You're a lovely big pig now!"

That day, after breakfast, Poppy went for a little walk round the farm, to make sure that she would be hungry enough for lunch. She trotted down to the duck pond and had a little drink and a chat with the ducklings. Then she wandered over to the henhouse and shared a mouthful of corn with the day-old chicks. Later, Poppy was trotting past one of the barns when she saw a hole in the side. Peering inside she saw a sack of carrots, a sack of turnips and a sack of onions. "Ooooh!" Poppy Pig sighed. "All my very favourite vegetables!"

Poppy pushed her head through the hole, then her shoulders and with a SQUIRM, a SQUEEZE and a GRUNT she was inside the barn. "Yummy!" she said to herself, "I think I'll just have a couple of carrots." So she did... then she had a couple of turnips...then she had some onions. "Mmmmm! Lovely!" she said, looking back at the carrots. "I think I might just try a few more of those!"

Poppy finished her 'snack' and thought she should hurry back to the pig sty, or she might be late for lunch! But when she tried to get out of the hole...SQUIRM... SQUEEZE...GRUNT... she couldn't!

She was stuck fast! She'd eaten so many carrots, turnips and onions that her tummy wouldn't go through the hole in the barn. "Oh dear! I think I might have grown into too much of a lovely big pig," thought Poppy to herself. And there she stayed. She missed lunch. She missed dinner and she missed breakfast, before she was thin enough to wriggle out again.

Pongo's Big Bone

Pongo was the littlest of all the puppies and never got any important jobs to do. Everyone else was always chosen to do things and he was left sitting by himself, with only his tail to play with. "Are you sure I can't help?" he'd ask his dad. "No, Son," his father would always reply, "you're too little."

Then one summer afternoon when everyone was lying in the warm sun, Pongo's dad said "I'd like to have a chew on my bone - would someone go and fetch it for me, please?" Pongo's ears pricked up "I'll go! I'll go!" he said eagerly, his little tail wagging like mad. "Let me go, Dad!" His dad smiled and nodded. "It's in my kennel, Pongo - but don't be too long now."

Pongo hurried off feeling very important indeed - he'd got a job to do at last! Rushing round to the kennels, he jumped over the ditch, squeezed through the fence, squirmed under the henhouse. There, outside the kennel,

lying next to the water bowl was the biggest bone he'd ever seen in his life. "Wow!" thought Pongo, "looks like it used to belong to a dinosaur!"

He stood at the middle of the enormous bone, got a good grip with his sharp little teeth, picked it up and staggered away. Getting to the hen house, he soon realised that he couldn't squirm underneath it carrying the enormous bone, so he had to go all the way round. Then he reached the fence. There was no way through, not with the enormous bone in his mouth, so he had to go right around the field. At the far side, he reached the ditch. Poor little

Pongo couldn't leap across, not with the enormous bone in his mouth, so he had to wade across.

At last when he reached his father, Little Pongo was tired out and panting, wet through and covered in mud. "Well done, Pongo," said his father. "Perhaps you're not too little after all."

The Last Egg

Mother Hen was feeling very pleased with herself. She'd laid six of the most perfect eggs anyone in the farmyard had ever seen! There were two lovely white eggs, three pretty speckled ones and a single large brown one. Mother Hen was sure she was going to have six beautiful chicks when all the eggs hatched.

When the day finally arrived, Mother Hen sat and watched as she began to hear tap-tap-tapping noises coming from inside the eggs.

Then, one by one, she saw little cracks appear and soon she was clucking proudly around five beautiful little chicks. She waited and she waited, but the sixth egg remained silent and refused to hatch. "Oh well," she said to herself, "better luck next time..."

Mother Hen took her five precious little chicks outside to show them to the rest of the animals and left the last egg all alone in the nest. Everyone thought the chicks were just the loveliest, fluffiest little things in the whole world, and made a huge fuss of them.

Meanwhile back inside the henhouse something was happening - the last egg - the single big brown one was starting to move. If you listened very carefully you could hear a faint tap...tap...tapping, coming from inside. The egg began to rock back and forth, faster and faster until it toppled out of the nest, rolled out of the door...down the ramp and out across the farmyard.

As the big brown egg stopped right by Mother Hen, its shell broke open.

"Goodness me!" said Mother Hen, as she looked down and saw the prettiest, fluffiest, yellowest chick of them all, looking up at her.
"My last chick!" she cried, as her sixth chick cheeped and went to join its brothers and sisters.

The Lamb Who Didn't Listen

"Now Lotty," said her mother, "I've got to go with the rest of the sheep, as it's time for us to have our lovely long wool clipped off for the summer. You be a good little lamb and stay here in the field and play with your friends."

Lotty didn't want to stay in the field with the rest of the lambs, that was boring. "Why can't I come with you? I want to be clipped, too!" she pleaded. Lotty's mother told her she was too little and too young to be clipped.

Before Lotty could say anything else, Rufus the sheepdog had rounded her mother up with the rest of the sheep. Before they went, Rufus the sheepdog turned to the little lamb and said, "listen to your mother, she knows best."

"Humph! I'm not staying here," Lotty said to herself, looking around the flat, dull field. "I'm going to find something more exciting to do!" So off she went. It didn't take her long to find a gap in the wall around the field and she was soon off exploring.

After a while she suddenly heard a gruff voice behind her. "Well! Hello little lambikins...why are you so far from home?...Where is your mummy?" Lotty looked round and saw a big, fierce fox grinning down at her.

"I'm...I'm just going for a walk," she whimpered.

"Oh! You don't want to go for walks on your own around here," he said, licking his lips. "You just don't know who you're going to meet!"

Lotty stared at his big brown eyes and sharp, white teeth and wished she had listened to her mother and stayed in the field with the rest of the lambs.

The handsome fox, his big bushy tail swishing behind him, walked slowly towards the little lamb, who was shivering with fear. Suddenly there was a loud bark, as Rufus the sheepdog leaped over the wall like a rocket! The fox turned tail and was gone in a flash.

"Little lambs should always listen to their mothers," said Rufus the sheepdog, "I'll take you back to your field right away." And do you know, from that day on, little Lotty Lamb always did everything that her mother said.

Patch Jumps For Joy

Patch the pony lived in a field on the farm with Joy the white mare, and Digby, an old carthorse. It was a big field that sloped down to a pond, but the pond was fenced off, because the farmer said it was too dangerous.

Every day, the Farmer's daughter would come to take Patch for a little ride. He would trot, canter and gallop, but there was one thing he would never do - Patch the pony would not jump!

One day in summer the sun was blazing down. Patch, Joy and Digby gazed down at the pond, filled with cool, cool water and longed for a nice paddle. "Push the fence over for me, Digby," asked Joy. "Don't think I should," replied the old carthorse. "Farmer wouldn't be very pleased." "Oh! Please, Digby," pleaded Joy.

So old Digby leant on the fence post. He was an enormous horse and the fence post soon snapped with a crack!

Joy stepped over the broken fence and began to wade into the cool water. "Come on in, it's wonderful," she called. But just then she felt her hooves sinking into the soft mud. "Help! Help! I'm sinking," she cried.

"We must go and warn the farmer," said Digby, "but the gate's closed." Little Patch looked back at Joy struggling in the pond, as she sunk deeper and deeper. Then he looked at the gate. It was a big, high gate, almost as high as his head. Without saying a word he galloped straight towards the big gate. Old Digby was amazed as he saw the little pony sail right over the big gate and race off towards the farm.

Moments later the farmer arrived in his tractor and quickly pulled poor Joy out of the sticky mud. Little Patch had saved his friend and he was never afraid of jumping again. In fact, Patch the pony now has rows of prizes for jumping pinned up on his stable wall.

The Cat Who Liked Mice!

Farmer Brown didn't believe Caspar was trying, so he told his wife, "until that cat starts to catch mice, he isn't allowed back in the house."

The next thing Caspar knew, he was out in the cold and wet and the door was banged shut behind him. Across the farmyard was a draughty old barn where he would now have to sleep.

"There's only one reason to have a cat on a farm," thundered Farmer Brown, "and that's to catch mice!" Mrs Brown looked down at Caspar the cat, sleeping peacefully on the rug by the fire. "I'm sure he tries his best, dear," she said. But the truth was, Caspar didn't try at all. In fact Caspar the cat liked mice.